The Hanging Book

The HANGING BOOK

by Bob Nilson

Foreword by Ogden Nash

Holt, Rinehart and Winston
NEW YORK   CHICAGO   SAN FRANCISCO

Dedicated to my father
Captain Alfred W. Nilson
of the Chinese junk *Amoy*

Copyright © 1970 by Robert Nilson

All rights reserved, including the right to reproduce
this book or portions thereof in any form.
Published simultaneously in Canada by Holt, Rinehart
and Winston of Canada, Limited.

Library of Congress Catalog Card Number: 70-103552

FIRST EDITION

SBN: 03-084412-6

Printed in the United States of America

Foreword

IT was Chesterton who in "A Ballade of Suicide" decided not to hang himself today. Among his ostensible reasons for the postponement were a) his uncle's sword was hanging in the hall; b) he saw a little cloud all pink and gray; c) perhaps the rector's mother would not call; and d) he had heard from a Mr. Gall that mushrooms could be cooked another way. Tush! I suspect that the truth is less complex; the poet simply mistrusted the ability of the rope to sustain his imposing bulk, and dreaded a fiasco in full view of his neighbors on the wall who were drawing a long breath to shout "Hurray!"

Chesterton was a humorist as well as a crusader and consequently recognized the ludicrous futility of man's agelong struggle against the inanimate, be it the rubbing stick that won't produce a flame, the windshield wiper that won't wipe, or the Scotch tape that won't let go of your finger. It is only the knowledge of this futility that has kept many a humorist from the sin of self-destruction. How often, confronted by solemn numskulls who condescendingly ask them when they are going to do something really worthwhile, have they contemplated the act. But these are men whose shoelaces won't stay laced, whose bow ties always come out lopsided, whose bedsheets will cover either their chins or their toes but not both, and the caps to whose tubes of toothpaste are forever vanishing down the drain of the basin; they are well aware that for them the bullet aimed at the temple will merely nick the ear, the poison lead only to the stomach pump, and the hemp to the sort of situation in which Nilson's frustrated *felos-de-se* find themselves. It is because instinct and experience have taught him that the inanimate exceeds even the human in perversity that history records no instance of a humorist's having perished by his own hand.

Not so with the Nilson characters. I see them as chillingly humorless and disgustingly efficient. They have always been able to change a tire, to locate and replace a burnt-out fuse, to free an impacted zipper on a lady's gown, and to insert Fig. 1 into Fig. 2 on the unassembled toy airplane. Anything we poor fumblers can't do they can do standing on their heads and whistling "Dixie," a fact too frequently noted and commented on by our wives.

Who would have thought to find these Leonardos, these Edisons, these Von Brauns, masters of the electric can-opener, the power lawn-mower and the granny-knot, denied a dramatic exit from this world by the recalcitrance of a paltry few yards of clothesline? Being humane, I am pleased by their survival; being human, I am delighted that their survival is ignominious. I am more than grateful to Bob Nilson for giving them their comedownance.

Ogden Nash

Introduction

WHY I chose attempted-suicide-by-hanging as the theme for a cartoon book will be explained in detail in my forthcoming book, *The Psychology of Humor.* But I would like to comment briefly here on why I decided on such a painful topic for humor.

After a long study of the psychology of laughter, I set about to synthesize humor, according to psychological principles. *The Hanging Book* is the first result. It is based on the psychological premise that events, of themselves, are neutral in effect. Only a viewer can (by reason of his attitude) call an event tragic or comic. That is, both tragedy and comedy (like beauty) lie in the eye of the beholder. The words tragic and comic pertain to our feelings about an event and are not inherent in the event. From this comes the truism that tragedy and comedy are but two sides of the same coin. It is also true that some events are more important to us than others and generate more of an emotional charge when perceived. It was just because the question of death is so important that I chose it as a topic. Death, when taken lightly, is after all terribly funny.

Many people helped to make this book possible. But I am happily indebted to no one more than Ogden Nash.

Bob Nilson

January, 1970

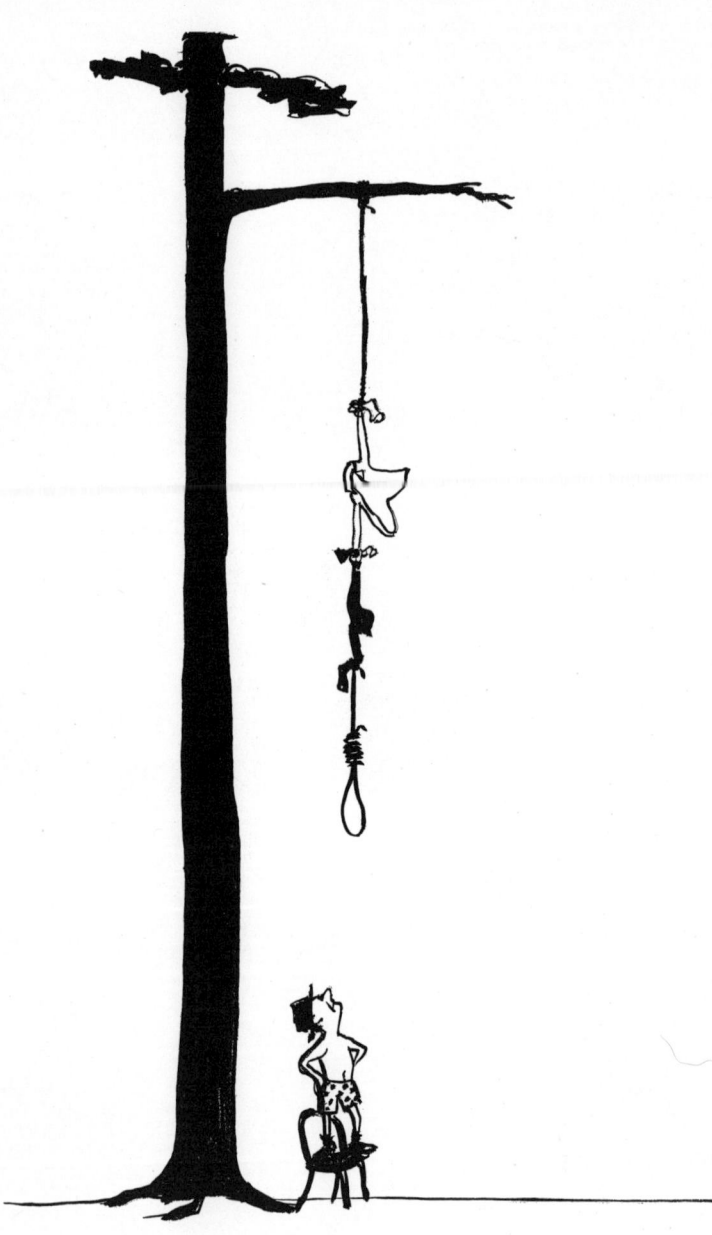

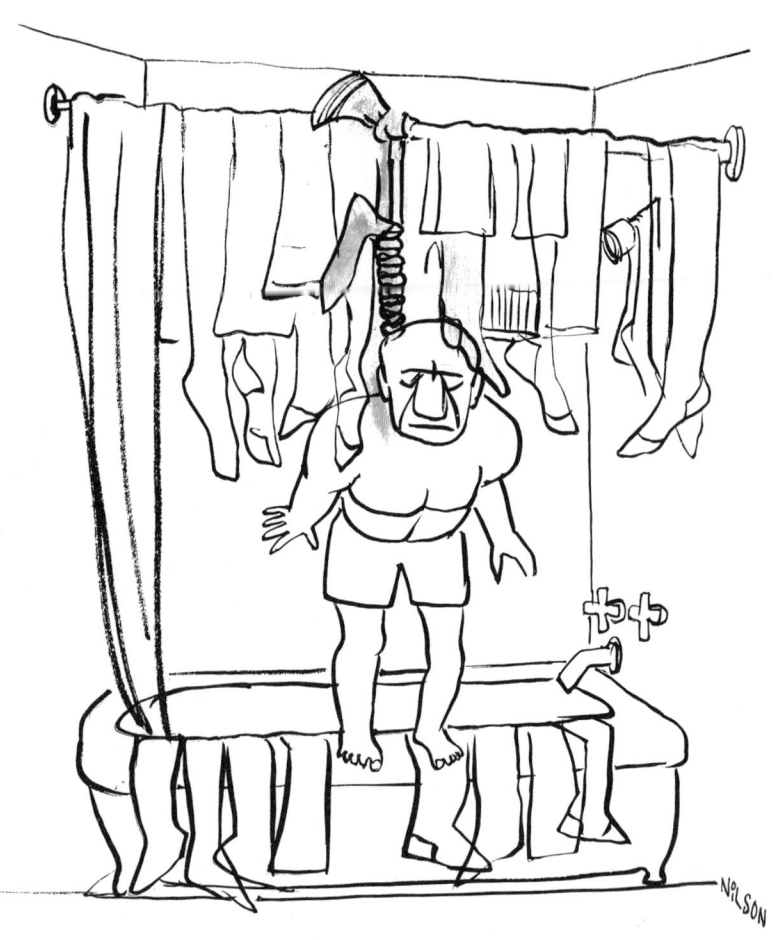

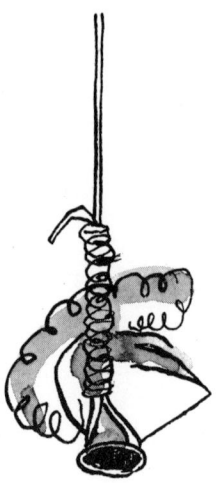
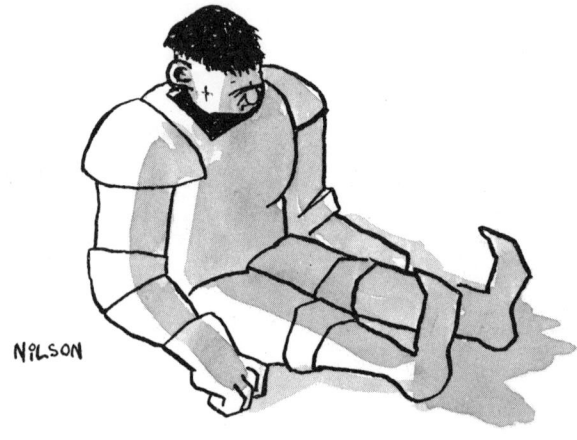

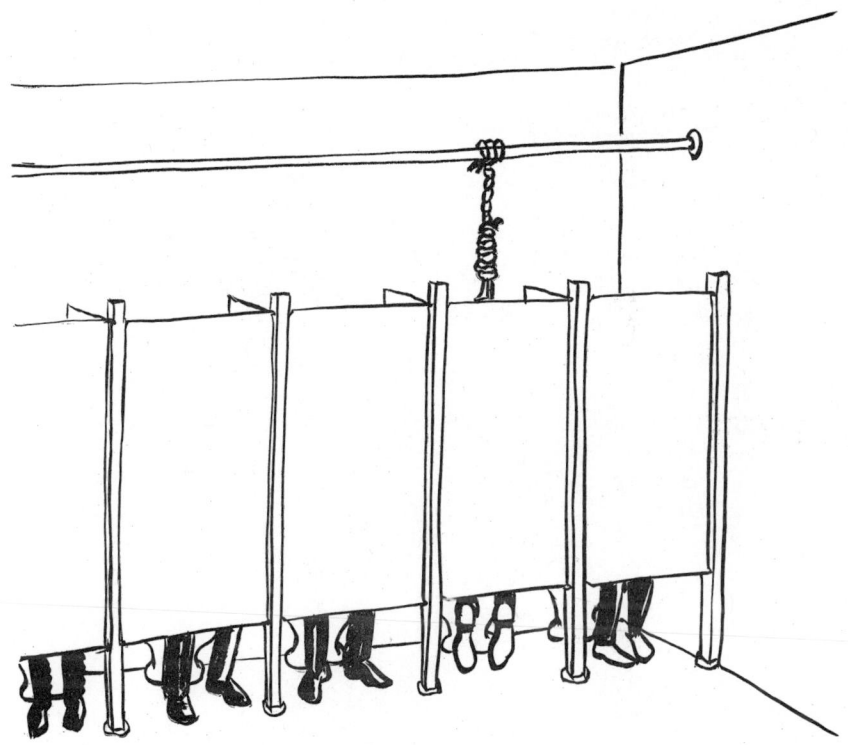

About the Artist

Bob Nilson developed a sense of humor while growing up aboard the Chinese junk *Amoy*, "first junk in the Atlantic Ocean." In New York he attended Cartoonists and Illustrators School, worked briefly in an ad agency, free-lanced cartoons, and then left for New Hampshire where his cartoons appeared regularly in several papers while he attended graduate schools. Mr. Nilson has taught classes at the New Hampshire University and at several New Hampshire colleges including what, he thinks, is the only course taught on The Psychology of Humor.

A member of New Hampshire Artists Association, Mr. Nilson's work has appeared in *Esquire, Playboy* and the *New Yorker.* Among his forthcoming books are *Man and Head* (cartoons), and *The Psychology of Humor,* a text.